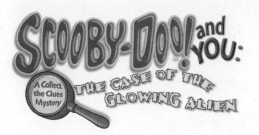

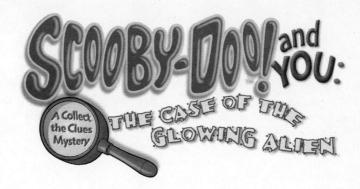

By James Gelsey

SCHOLASTIC INC.

New York   Toronto   London   Auckland   Sydney
Mexico City   New Delhi   Hong Kong

ISBN 0-439-21750-4

12 11 10 9 8 7 6 5 4 3 2 1   0 1 2 3 4 5/0

Cover and interior illustrations by Duendes del Sur
Cover and interior design by Madalina Stefan

Printed in the U.S.A.

First Scholastic printing, September 2000

For Sue

"Hey, come on over!" Fred calls from across the pizza parlor. "It's great to see you."

You close the door to Louie's Pizza Parlor. It's warm inside, and the smell of freshly baked pizza fills the place. You walk over to the big booth in the back where Fred, Velma, Daphne, Shaggy, and Scooby are sitting. Shaggy and Scooby each have a big pile of pizza crusts in front of them.

"Are you ready, Scoob?" Shaggy asks.

"*Ready!*" Scooby says, smiling.

"On the count of three," Shaggy continues. "One. Two. Wait — hold it!" Shaggy looks at you.

"Like, do you wanna join our crust crunching contest?" he asks you.

"Shaggy, we'd like to talk to our friend, if you don't mind," Daphne interrupts.

"Gee, Daph, I was just being friendly," Shaggy replies. "Okay, Scoob, where was I?"

"*Ree!*" Scooby exclaims as he starts devouring the pizza crusts.

"Hey, no fair!" Shaggy yells. Then he starts gobbling up the pizza crusts, too.

"Don't mind them," Velma says. "They've been talking about their crust crunching contest all day."

"All week is more like it," Daphne adds. "Ever since we got back from solving our last mystery."

"And that was some mystery," Fred says. "It was unlike any we've ever had to solve."

You're having a hard time paying attention to Fred, Daphne, and Velma. Shaggy and Scooby are crunching up a storm, and bits of pizza crust are flying everywhere.

"Mmmmumph," Shaggy says with a mouthful of pizza crust.

"What did you say?" Daphne asks.

"Mmm...mummph!" Shaggy says, trying to swallow his mouthful of food.

"You really shouldn't talk with your mouth full," Velma lectures. "It's bad for your digestion."

"I think he's trying to say —" Fred begins.

"*Rinished!*" Scooby says, licking his lips. His plate is clean and his mouth is empty.

"Mumph!" Shaggy says, still working on the food in his mouth.

You smile and congratulate Scooby, giving him a pat on the head.

"Now about that mystery," Fred says. "We sure could've used your help."

"I bet you would've been able to figure it out in no time," Velma says.

Just the thought of solving a mystery brings a smile to your face.

"Judging by your expression," Daphne says, "I think you'd love the chance to solve the mystery, right?"

"You bet!" you say.

"That's great!" Fred says. "Because it just so happens that you can. This is our Clue Keeper for the case."

Fred holds up a small notebook with a patterned cover.

"We call this mystery *The Case of the Glowing Alien*," Fred says as he hands you the notebook.

"We write down everything that happens to us in our Clue Keeper," Daphne explains. "The people we meet, the clues we find, you know, things like that."

"We take turns writing the journal," Fred adds. "I was the writer for this mystery."

"All you have to do is read our Clue Keeper," Velma continues. "We've even added some shortcuts. Whenever you see

this  you know you've met a suspect in the case. And whenever you see this you've found a clue."

"Our Clue Keeper is divided into sections," Fred says. "At the end of some entries, we'll ask you questions. This will help you organize the suspects and clues you find. All you need is your own Clue Keeper and a pen or pencil."

"So, what do you say?" Daphne asks. "Are you ready?"

5

Before you can answer, Shaggy interrupts.

"So, Scooby, how about two out of three?" he asks.

"*Ro rore room,*" Scooby says, shaking his head and pating his belly.

Shaggy then looks at you. "Like, I'll bet you're up to a crust crunching contest, right?" he asks.

"Not now, Shaggy," Fred says. "I think our friend has something a little more important to do. Right?"

You nod your head in excitement.

"Right!" you exclaim.

Clue Keeper Entry 1

The gang and I arrived at High Point Park for a big picnic celebrating the park's opening. The park sits on top of a large hill, making it the highest point in the county. The park used to be an old dump. Then some people decided to volunteer their time to clean it up.

A lot of people were there that afternoon enjoying the view from the observation platform. Others were playing catch on the great lawn in front of the main pavilion. And still others were there for the food.

"So, like, where's the barbecue?" Shaggy asked.

"Right over there, young man," a woman replied.

It was Cecilia Cornwallis. She's the one who organized all of the volunteers. Cecilia was a tall woman dressed all in green. She wore a yellow scarf tied around her neck.

"The park looks beautiful," Daphne said. "You'd never know what used to be up here."

"Yes, I'm very proud of this park," Cecilia told us. "But I am worried that it may not last very long."

"Why not?" Velma asked.

"Since this was a volunteer effort, we need the town's approval to make it an official park," Cecilia explained. "But there are a lot of people who want the land to be used for other things. I'm afraid that if anything goes wrong today, one of them might just get their way."

"And I'll bet dollars to donuts it'll be me," said a man walking by. He stopped and joined our conversation. "But don't worry, darling. I'll give you full credit. Directed by Sy Stroganoff. Set Design by Cecilia

Cornwallis and her volunteer clean-up brigade." The man laughed.

"Don't laugh, Sy," Cecilia warned. "You may not get your way. And if I have anything to say about it, no one will."

"We'll see, Cecilia," the man said. He turned to us and introduced himself. "I'm Sy Stroganoff. Pleased to meet you."

"Sy Stroganoff?" Shaggy said. "Like, you directed Scooby's and my favorite movie: *Attack of the Crazy Pizza Man.*"

"Ah, one of my early classics," Sy said.

"What brings you to High Point Park?" I asked.

"I'm here to direct a movie," Sy said. "This park is the perfect setting. Of course, we'll need to put in some cactus plants. And tear up some of the grass."

"You wouldn't," Cecilia said.

"I probably will," Sy replied. "Especially once the town council realizes how much money and tourism my film will bring to this place."

"Uh, Ms. Cornwallis, you don't look so

well," Daphne said. "Would you like some water or something?"

"A very good idea," Cecilia said. "Please, excuse me." Cecilia walked away.

"Like, what kind of movie are you making, Mr. Stroganoff?" Shaggy asked. *"Return of the Crazy Pizza Man?"*

"No," Sy replied. "It's a special movie that requires the unique characteristics of this beautiful park."

"Is it about nature?" Velma asked.

"No, aliens," Sy said. "With lots of special effects. We've even started running wires and things in the trees. They're part of our special effects, you see. Now if you'll excuse me, I must go to the effects trailer and check on the latest version of the alien."

Once Sy Stroganoff walked away, Shaggy said, "Like, I think Scooby and I are ready for a little barbecue. What do you say, pal?"

"Rou ret!" agreed Scooby.

Shaggy and Scooby walked over to the food while Daphne, Velma and I went to check out the view.

Velma's Mystery-Solving Tips

"Hey, did you notice the 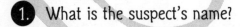 back on page 10? That was a tip that you've found your first suspect. Now grab your Clue Keeper and answer the following questions about this suspect."

1. What is the suspect's name?

2. What kind of work does he do?

3. And why is he so interested in the park?

12

Clue Keeper Entry 2

Shaggy and Scooby walked across the grass toward the barbecues.

"Hey, Scoob, remember that scene from *Attack of the Crazy Pizza Man*?" Shaggy asked. "You know, the one where the Crazy Pizza Man splashes tomato sauce over everybody? They sure don't make movies like that anymore, right, pal? Scooby?"

Shaggy realized that Scooby wasn't paying attention. Scooby was watching a small animal scurry across the grass.

"Scooby, that's just a squirrel," Shaggy said.

"*Ratch ris*," Scooby whispered to Shaggy. Scooby crouched down and crawled very slowly across the grass on his stomach. Just as he was about to stand up and shout "boo!" two men came running over.

"Hey! Stop!" they yelled. The squirrel looked up at Scooby. It made a screeching sound so loud that Scooby had to cover his ears. Then the squirrel jumped up onto Scooby's back. From there, it jumped onto a tree and ran up the trunk, disappearing into the branches. Shaggy ran over to the tree as the two men got there.

"We're sorry we yelled at you," one of them said.

"But we didn't want you to hurt the squirrel," the other added. "They can get upset quite easily."

"Like, are there really two people there?" Shaggy whispered to Scooby. "Or am I seeing double?"

The two men, it turned out, were identical twins.

"We're the Bell Brothers," the other said.

"I'm Don, and this Ron. We run the local animal shelter." 👁 👁

"So, like, what's the big deal about the
squirrel?" Shaggy asked.

"That was no ordinary squirrel," Ron answered. "It was a red-bellied sap squirrel."

"The red-bellied sap squirrel is a very rare
breed," Don explained. "It's almost extinct,
in fact."

Ron continued, "And this park is the only
red-bellied sap squirrel habitat left in this
part of the country."

"We've spent a lot of time and money trying to protect these squirrels and their habi-tat," Don said. "We've put monitoring equip-ment all over the park so we can keep track of them. Look up in that tree there."

Don pointed to a small black box hidden among the branches of the tree.

"We're trying to get this park turned into a nature preserve," Don continued. "So the squirrels will have a safe place to live."

"We've even strung wires between the treetops," Ron said. "That way the squirrels can get around without having to walk on the ground. That keeps them safe from their natural enemies."

"Like, who would that be?" Shaggy asked.

"Well, people for one," Ron answered. "They trample in the nuts and berries that the squirrels eat." Then he looked right at Scooby. "But dogs are an even greater threat."

"We submitted a petition to the town council," Don said. "But even if they don't approve it, we'll keep on fighting."

"Don, over there!" Ron said. "Someone's

about to feed a squirrel. Come on!" Ron ran off, followed by Don.

"Speaking of feeding," Shaggy said. "Like, let's go find that barbecue. We still have time for a pre-dinner snack."

Shaggy and Scooby's Mystery-Solving Tips

"Like, did you see the 👀 on page 15? Groovy. Now open your Clue Keeper and answer the following questions about this entry."

1. What are the suspects' names?

2. What kind of work do they do?

3. Like, why are they so interested in the park? "Now go and have a snack!"

Clue Keeper Entry 3

Daphne, Velma, and I stood along the observation platform at one end of the park. The sun was just beginning to set. We looked out over miles and miles of hills and trees.

"Jinkies," Velma exclaimed. "I wonder how far you can see from up here."

"On a clear day you can see for twenty-seven miles," a man said. I looked over and saw a man standing with a telescope.

"Twenty-seven miles straight ahead," the man said. "But thousands of miles straight up." He pointed to the sky.

"Straight up?" Daphne asked. "Hey, are you an astronomer?"

"That's right. My name's Greg Grogan," the man said. "There's no other place like this for miles. You know, I've been begging the town to build an observatory here for years."

"Then you must be happy that this park finally opened," I said.

"Oh, no, no, no," Greg replied. "The last thing I want is a park here. No, what this town needs is a state-of-the-art observatory for mapping other galaxies, and finding comets, and looking for life in space."

"Did you say life in space?" Velma asked.

"Of course," Greg said. "There have been no less than seventeen UFO sightings up here alone. I've seen six of them myself."

I looked at the girls. They looked at me. I could tell they were thinking what I was thinking — this guy was a bit odd to say the least.

"I know what you're thinking," Greg said. "I'm just another loony who's looking for aliens. But mark my words, those aliens will show up and prove I'm right. Before you know it, you'll be looking at the Gregory Grogan Observatory right here. Now if you'll excuse me, I have to find a certain star before the fireworks start."

We had forgotten about the big fireworks show scheduled for that evening. We made our quick good-byes to Greg Grogan and headed back to the center of the park.

"He gave me the creeps," Daphne said.

"Like, did you meet those crazy brothers, too?" Shaggy asked. He and Scooby walked up to the girls and me. They were finishing their barbecue snacks.

"What brothers?" Velma asked. "We were talking about Greg Grogan, that guy looking through the telescope."

"Scooby and I just ran into these two creepy twin brothers," Shaggy said. "Like, they thought Scooby was going to hurt one of their red-bellied sap squirrels."

"That's odd," said Velma.

"Like, I know," Shaggy agreed. "I mean, everybody knows my pal here would never hurt a squirrel. Right, Scoob?"

"Right!" Scooby said.

"No, Shaggy, I mean about the red-bellied sap squirrels," Velma continued. "I've never heard of that kind of squirrel."

"Well, don't tell those brothers," Shaggy said. "They want to turn the park into a nature preserve just to protect them."

"It sounds to me like Cecilia Cornwallis has a lot of reasons to be worried about the park," I said.

"I just hope everything turns out okay," Daphne said.

"Of course it will, Daph," Shaggy said. "Like, what could possibly go wrong?"

Fred and Daphne's
Mystery-Solving Tips

"Did you catch the  on page 20? Fred and I thought you would. Grab your Clue Keeper and answer the following questions about this suspect."

1. What is the suspect's name?

2. What kind of work does he do?

3. Why is he so interested in the park?

Clue Keeper Entry 4

By this time, it was dark outside. Everyone had gathered on the great lawn in the center of the park for the fireworks show. The gang and I sat down on the grass and waited for the show to begin. One by one, the lights on the lampposts started going out.

"Huh?" Scooby asked.

"Don't worry, Scooby," Daphne said. "They're just turning out the lampposts so we can see the fireworks better, that's all."

"*Rokay*," Scooby said with relief.

Then a funny sound filled the air.

"Like, I've heard some weird music be-fore," Shaggy said, "but this is the weirdest."

A moment later, a bright light descended from the sky. As it got lower, the strange sound got louder. Suddenly, there was a big flash of light and a huge puff of smoke. The crowd started getting scared.

"I wonder what's going on?" Velma asked.

"Could it be . . . a . . . a . . . spaceship?" Shaggy asked, shaking with fear.

Then, from out of nowhere, a strange looking creature appeared to fly through the air. It had a small round head and long arms with very skinny fingers. And its skin seemed to glow in the dark. The alien started making a strange and scary sound. It was so loud, Scooby had to cover his ears.

"Zoinks! It's a space alien!" Shaggy yelled. "Everybody run!"

The other people sitting on the lawn stood up and ran away screaming. The alien flew back and forth making all kinds of strange sounds. Then it suddenly disap-peared.

As people ran out of the park, Cecilia

Cornwallis walked around trying to calm them down. Soon, the gang, Ms. Cornwallis and I were the only ones left.

"I can't believe it," Cecilia said. "Once word spreads about this, they'll close the park for sure. Who would want to come to a park that is haunted by aliens?"

"Wow!" Daphne exclaimed. "Do you think that Greg Grogan could have been right about intelligent life in outer space?"

26

"I don't know about outer space," I said. "But I do know there's intelligent life right here on Earth. And I think we need to use it to figure out if this alien is for real."

"Fred's right," Daphne said.

"Ms. Cornwallis?" I asked. "Don't worry about a thing. The Mystery, Inc. gang is on the case."

"Thank you, kids," Cecilia said. "Is there anything I can do to help?"

27

"You can start by turning the lampposts back on," Velma said. "We'll need every bit of light to help us search for clues."

"Would you happen to have any flashlights?" Daphne asked.

"In my car," Cecilia answered. "I'll get them right after I turn the lampposts back on."

"When Cecilia returns with the flashlights, we'll split up to look for clues," Fred said.

Clue Keeper Entry 5

Cecilia Cornwallis returned with four flashlights.

"Thanks, Ms. Cornwallis," Daphne said. "Do you want to join us?"

"No, thank you," Cecilia replied. "I'm still a bit shaken up about the whole thing. I'm going to rest in the main pavilion. Come get me as soon as you find something."

"Daphne and I will check out the other side of the park," I said. "You know, where the spaceship seemed to land."

"Great idea," Velma said. "Shaggy, Scooby and I will look around here for signs of the alien."

29

"We'll meet back at the main pavilion," I said. "Now let's get started," Fred said. Daphne and I walked off across the great lawn.

"I noticed that the alien only moved between those two tall trees," Velma said. She pointed toward a couple of trees on the opposite side of the lawn.

"Shaggy, Scooby, you two check out that tree," Velma instructed. "I'll look on the other side. If you find anything suspicious, flash your flashlight quickly three times." Velma walked to the other side of the great lawn.

Shaggy shined his flashlight out in front of him and Scooby. They walked quickly to the tree.

"I don't see anything here," Shaggy said. "Do you, Scoob?"

"*Uh-uh,*" Scooby said.

"Oh, well, that's the way it goes," Shaggy said. "At least we tried. What do you say we head back to the pavilion and see if we can get something to eat."

"*Right!*" Scooby said. Shaggy and Scooby

turned and walked toward the main pavilion. On their way, a flashing light caught their attention.

"Like, I think Velma's found something," Shaggy said. They changed direction and walked across the lawn to Velma. She was standing next to a tree. She shined her flashlight up into the branches.

"Tell me what you see," Velma said.

Shaggy and Scooby looked up.

"Like, a tree, Velma," Shaggy replied.

"No, where my light is shining," Velma said.

"*Reaves*," Scooby answered.

"And branches," Shaggy added.

"Don't you see that small black box up on the branch?" Velma asked. "It's right there."

Shaggy and Scooby looked up again.

"Oh, yeah," Shaggy said. "It looks like a miniature stereo speaker."

"Doesn't that strike you as odd?" Velma asked.

Shaggy thought for a moment.

"Yeah, I guess so," Shaggy said. "Like, why would squirrels be listening to music?" Shaggy said to Scooby.

"My point exactly," Velma said.

"I mean, squirrels don't even have ears," Shaggy continued.

"Oh, brother," Velma said, rolling her eyes at Shaggy's response. "I'm going to see if there are small black boxes in other trees."

"Great," Shaggy said. "Scooby and I will go check out the snack bar — I mean, go meet Fred and Daphne at the main pavilion."

"Just be careful, you two," Velma warned.

"No sweat, Velma," Shaggy said. "Like, we're just walking across the lawn to the main pavilion. What could possibly happen to us between here and there?"

Velma's
Mystery-Solving Tips

"**D**id you notice the  on page 32? That's where you'll find your first clue. Open up your Clue Keeper and answer the following questions about it."

1. What clue did you find in this entry?

2. What do you think this clue has to do with the alien?

3. Which of the suspects could have left this clue?

Clue Keeper Entry 6

Shaggy and Scooby walked across the grass toward the main pavilion.

"Like, did you hear something, Scoob?" Shaggy asked.

Scooby tilted his head and raised his left ear. Then he slowly moved his head from left to right.

"*Uh-uh*," Scooby reported.

"Must be my imagination," Shaggy said. "For a second, I thought I heard the Crazy Pizza Man following us."

Shaggy and Scooby looked at each other. Then they started walking a little faster.

"Scooby, quit walking so close to me,"

Shaggy complained. "Like, your breath is melting the back of my neck."

"*Rorry,*" Scooby said. Shaggy looked over and saw that Scooby was walking next to him, not behind him.

"Uh, Scoob, since you're not following me," whispered Shaggy. "Can you tell me, like, who is following me?"

Scooby looked at Shaggy and then behind him.

"*Ralien!*" Scooby yelled.

"Zoinks!" Shaggy echoed. "Run, Scoob!"

The alien chased Shaggy and Scooby all the way to the main pavilion. It made terrible screeching sounds. Shaggy and Scooby tried to run inside the main pavilion, but the door was locked. When they turned to run the other way, they noticed the alien was gone.

"Hey, like, he's gone, Scoob," Shaggy said.

Shaggy and Scooby heard someone's footsteps in the grass. They saw some kind of light getting closer.

"Zoinks! It's back!" Shaggy cried. "He's

gonna melt our eyeballs and turn us into rocks! Good-bye, Scoob, old pal." Shaggy closed his eyes tightly. After a minute or two, he opened his right eye to see where the alien was. Daphne and I were standing in front of him.

"Would you mind telling us what you are doing, Shaggy?" Daphne asked.

"Like, the alien chased me and Scooby," Shaggy said.

"Where's Velma?" I asked.

"She was looking for more clues," Shaggy said. "Like, I hope the alien didn't get her."

"We should probably go find her," Daphne said.

"Good idea, Daphne," I said. "Let's go, fellas."

"Oh, no you don't," Shaggy said. "We're not going out there where some alien can chase us and beam its death ray at us."

"Okay," Daphne said. "I just hope that the alien doesn't come back here looking for you two!" She and I walked away.

"*Rait ror rus!*" Scooby called as he and Shaggy ran after us.

As Shaggy and Scooby ran, they sud-

denly tripped on something and went flying into one another. Daphne and I stopped.

"Would you two quit clowning around?" Daphne asked.

"Like, something tripped us," Shaggy said.

"*Reah, ripped rus,*" Scooby agreed.

"Shaggy's right," Velma said. She walked out from behind a tree holding something. "I found this harness attached to a thin cable running between these two trees."

"A harness and cable?" Daphne asked. "What's that doing here?"

"It was used by our alien to appear to fly," Velma explained. "Only when I took the harness down, I accidentally unhooked the cable. That's what Shaggy and Scooby tripped on."

"And now you need to see what Daphne and I found," I said. "Come on."

"Like, Velma found another interesting clue by the  in this entry. Did you find it, too? Great. Now get your Clue Keeper and answer these questions about it. And, like, don't forget to give yourself another snack when you're done."

1. What clue did you find in this entry?

2. What do you think the clue has to do with the alien?

3. Which of the suspects could have put the cables up across the trees?

Clue Keeper Entry 7

The gang and I walked over to the far side of the great lawn. There were two big trees on opposite sides of the grass.

"Now watch closely," I said.

I walked over to one tree, and Daphne to the other.

"Ready, Daph?" I asked.

"Ready," she replied.

I reached up and pulled on a branch. Suddenly, a ball of colorful lights appeared near the top of the tree. The lights then started floating down.

"Zoinks!" Shaggy exclaimed. "It's the alien's spaceship."

"No, it's not, Shaggy," Velma said. "It's just a string of colored lights bunched together."

"I don't care what they are," Shaggy said. "They're flying!"

"Actually, the lights are attached to a very thin wire that extends from the top of that tree to the bottom of this one," Daphne said. "I'm pulling another wire that's making the lights move."

"So, like it's not a spaceship?" Shaggy asked. "That's a relief, right Scoob? Scoob?"

Scooby was holding something. He reached down and touched it with his paw. A loud screeching sound filled the air.

"*Rikes!*" Scooby howled. He jumped up and threw the thing to the ground.

"The alien!" Shaggy yelled.

Velma walked over to where the sound was coming from. She knelt down and picked something up. She pushed a button on it and the sound stopped.

"Scooby, where did you get that?" I asked.

"*Ron ruh rass,*" Scooby answered.

Velma looked at it carefully. "That's odd," she said. "This portable cassette player has a built-in loudspeaker."

"Yeah, emphasis on loud," Shaggy said.

"I'll bet the alien dropped it when he was chasing you earlier," Daphne said.

"Things are starting to fall into place," Velma said. "I have a hunch that this alien isn't from another town, much less another planet."

"Velma's right," I said. "It's time to set a trap."

"Daphne and I hope you saw the  on page 42, because this is an important clue. Make sure you answer all of the questions about it in your Clue Keeper."

1. What clue did you find in this entry?

2. What other time do you remember hearing a sound like this?

3. Which suspects were around when you heard that sound?

Clue Keeper Entry 8

The gang and I had a great idea for the trap: We were going to out-alien the alien. First, Velma and Daphne needed to disguise Scooby as an alien. Then Shaggy was supposed to get the alien to chase him across the great lawn. When the alien got to a certain spot, Scooby would fly through the air using the harness and wires that Velma found earlier. Once Scooby startled the alien, Shaggy and I would jump out and capture it in one of the picnic blankets left on the lawn. The only hard part was convincing Scooby-Doo.

"Please, Scooby?" Daphne said. "We'll give you a Scooby Snack."

"*Uh-uh,*" Scooby answered. He crossed his paws and looked away.

"Will you do it for two Scooby Snacks?" Velma asked.

"*Mmmmmm,*" Scooby thought for a moment. "Rope!"

"All right, three Scooby Snacks," Daphne said. "But that's it."

"*Rokay!*" said Scooby. Daphne and Velma took turns tossing the three Scooby Snacks into the air. Scooby jumped up and gobbled down each one.

We were finally able to spring into action. Daphne and Velma took Scooby aside and started putting together an alien disguise. I walked with Shaggy toward the main pavilion.

"Remember, Shaggy, just make sure you run to the right trees," I said.

45

"Like, I'm so scared that any tree where there isn't an alien is the right tree for me," Shaggy replied.

"Then don't think about the alien," I coaxed. "Pretend you're being chased by the Crazy Pizza Man instead."

"The Crazy Pizza Man?" Shaggy said. "No one's afraid of the Crazy Pizza Man. He's, like, made out of pizza crusts and burnt cheese."

"That's great, Shaggy," I said. "If you get scared, think of the Crazy Pizza Man." I turned and left Shaggy alone. Inside, I was holding my breath hoping that he wouldn't mess up the plans.

"Oh, I'm not scared," Shaggy called. "But thanks to all that talk about the Crazy Pizza Man, now I'm hungry."

Shaggy stood on the grass and looked around. It was pretty quiet.

"Hey, alien, come out, come out, from wherever you are," Shaggy called. "Like, maybe he flew back to his planet." Shaggy walked across the lawn. After a few steps,

Shaggy felt that same hot breath on the back of his neck.

"Gulp," Shaggy swallowed hard. He turned his head just a bit and caught a glimpse of a greenish face and long slender fingers.

"Zoinks!" Shaggy exlaimed. "Coming through!" Shaggy started running. The alien chased him all over the great lawn.

"Psssssst, Shaggy!" Daphne whispered from the trees. "This way!" She pointed toward the middle of the great lawn.

Shaggy started running in that direction.

Suddenly, a strange-looking creature flew out of nowhere and across the sky.

"Zoinks!" Shaggy yelled. "It's another one!" He turned and started running in the opposite direction. I quickly caught Shaggy's attention and waved him over behind a tree.

The alien who was chasing Shaggy saw the flying alien, who was really Scooby in disguise. Scooby then made some strange alien sounds.

"*Roooooooooo,*" Scooby moaned.

The alien stared at Scooby. It reached its hand up and tried to grab Scooby's foot.

"*Rikes!*" Scooby yelled.

Very quietly, Shaggy and I held a picnic blanket and snuck up behind the alien. Just as we were about to throw the blanket over the alien, we heard something snap. Shaggy had stepped on a branch.

The alien whipped around and let out a big screech, startling us. Suddenly, everyone heard the flying alien say, "*Roooooby-Rooby-Roo!*"

The alien looked up and saw Scooby unfasten his harness. Before the glowing alien could run away, Scooby landed right on top of him with a thud.

Cecilia Cornwallis ran across the lawn with Daphne and Velma.

"You've caught him!" Cecilia exclaimed. "How wonderful."

"Would you like to see who's behind all this?" Daphne asked.

"Absolutely, dear," Cecilia replied. She reached over and pulled the alien's mask right off his head.

"**H**ey, who ordered the spaghetti pizza?" Louie shouts from behind the counter.

You look up from reading the gang's Clue Keeper.

"Well, now you've met all the suspects and found all the clues," Fred says. "Do you think you're up to solving the mystery?"

You nod your head.

"Great," Daphne says. "Here's some advice. Look at your list of suspects and clues and answer these questions."

"First, who do you think had a good reason to scare people away from the park?" Velma asks.

"Second, who do you think had the know-how to scare people away from the park?" Fred asks.

"Third, who do you think had the opportunity to scare people away from the park?" Daphne asks.

"See if you can eliminate any of the suspects first," Velma suggests. "Then using all of the information you've collected, as well as your own smarts, try to figure out who the alien really is."

"Like, anybody want some?" Shaggy asks as Louie puts a huge plate in front of him and Scooby. "Louie makes the best spaghetti pizza around."

"Why don't you solve the mystery while Shaggy and Scooby are having their snack?" Daphne suggests. "Then when you're done, we'll tell you who was behind all the antics."

"Jinkies! It's your last chance to solve the mystery before the gang reveals the answer. When you're ready, turn the page to read the groovy ending of The Case of the Glowing Alien."

"The Bell Brothers were behind the whole thing," Velma says. "Don wore the alien costume, and Ron operated the fake spaceship and the lights and the pulleys to make Don fly."

"You know that our other two suspects were Greg Grogan, the amateur astronomer," Daphne says.

"And Sy Stroganoff," Fred adds. "All of the suspects had reasons for wanting to keep people away from the park."

"After thinking about it a bit, we decided Greg Grogan couldn't have had anything to do with the mystery," Daphne says. "After all, he's the only suspect who truly believed in intelligent life on other planets. He wouldn't want people to think that aliens were mean and scary."

"That left the Bell Brothers and Sy Stroganoff," Fred says. "They all had access to the park to put up wires and speakers and things."

"After all, Sy Stroganoff said he was already preparing for his movie shoot," Daphne says. "And the Bell Brothers said they put up monitors and cables for the squirrels."

"Mr. Stroganoff could have used his movie equipment to make the alien and all the effects," Fred explains. "Or the Bell Brothers could have used their monitors as loudspeakers and stolen the rest from Mr. Stroganoff's storage truck."

"The clue that tipped us off was the portable tape player that Scooby found," Velma says. "It was supposed to be the alien's voice. But the sound on that tape is definitely not from outer space. Right, Scooby?"

"*Right!*" agrees Scooby.

"The Bell Brothers had recorded the squirrel sounds and used them to make the alien's screeches," Daphne explains. "All in the name of preserving the red-bellied sap squirrel."

Just then, a red-bellied sap squirrel jumps up from under the table and sits next to the spaghetti pizza and Scooby. The squirrel takes a nibble of the pizza crust and screeches happily.

"And turning their nature preserve into an all-squirrel zoo that they hoped to make money on," Fred adds.

Everyone across the table now looks at you.

"So, how did you do?" Daphne asks.

"I'll bet you solved the mystery without any problem," Velma adds with a smile. "After all, you do have some pretty good teachers."

"Like, solving mysteries isn't all you can learn from us," Shaggy says to you.

"Really?" Daphne asks. "What else is there?"

"Like, the best way to eat a spaghetti pizza," Shaggy says.

He and Shaggy each take a huge bite of the spaghetti pizza. As they slurp up the spaghetti, you notice that they are eating opposite ends of the same piece. Shaggy and Scooby both try to slurp the spaghetti into their mouths. Suddenly, the red-bellied sap squirrel jumps up and takes a bite out of the middle. The ends of the spaghetti quickly disappear into Shaggy's and Scooby's mouths. The squirrel chews happily.

"Come back and visit us again," Fred says. "There's always another mystery to solve."

"And, like, another pizza to eat," Shaggy says. "Right, Scoob?"

"*Rooooooby-Rooby-Roo!*" Scooby agrees.